OE Want Be Friday

A True Story Promoting Inclusion and Self-Determination

Finding My Way Series

Jo Meserve Mach
Vera Lynne Stroup-Rentier

Photography by Mary Birdsell

BROWN BOOKS
PUBLISHING GROUP

OE Wants It to Be Friday.
A True Story Promoting Inclusion and Self-Determination

Brown Books Kids
16250 Knoll Trail Drive, Suite 205
Dallas, Texas 75248
www.BrownBooksKids.com
(972) 381-0009

A New Era in Publishing®

ISBN 978-1-61254-258-4
LCCN 2016913869

Printed in the United States
10 9 8 7 6 5 4 3 2 1

For more information or to contact the author, please go to
www.findingmywaybooks.com

Hi, my name is Olga Ellise.
Everyone calls me OE.
I have fun everyday.
But Friday is the best day of the week.

It's Monday.
There are four more days until Friday.
What should I wear?
It's fun to pick.

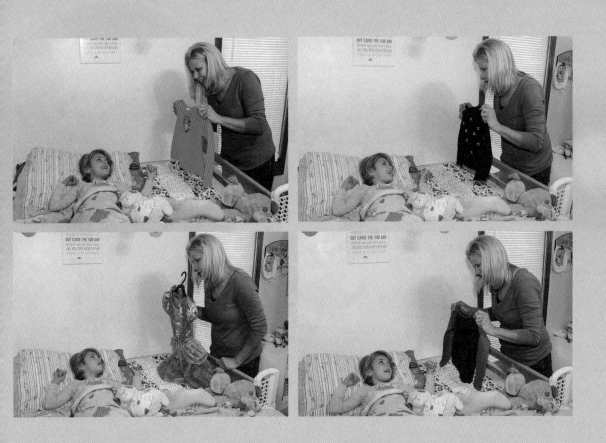

I shake my head.
No, that's too hot.
That's too dark.
That's too silly.
Now that's what I want to wear today.

It's Tuesday.
There are three more days until Friday.
Mom needs to go to the store.
I get to go with her.

Mom and I like to sing in the car.
Mom finds a song on the radio.

We're loud and silly.
I act like I'm a real singer.

It's Wednesday.
There are two more days until Friday.
My brother, Tyler, helps me study.
I have a spelling test on Friday.

Tonight is family game night.
My sister, Abbie, lets me pick the
game.

I love our family fun.
Mom, Dad, Hannah, Abbie and Tyler
are all playing with me.

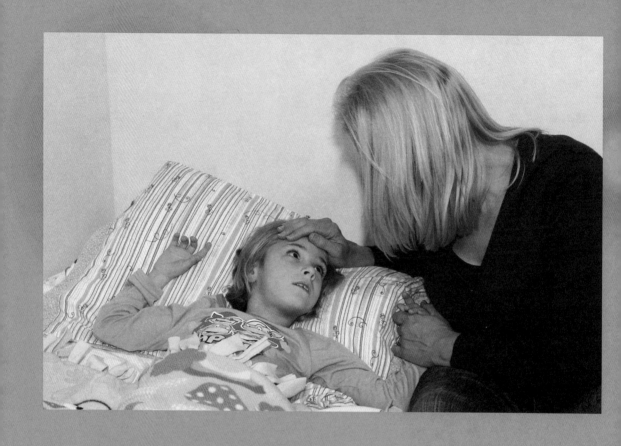

It's Thursday.
There's just one more day until Friday.
Oh, no! I feel hot.
Mom says I can't go to school.

I rest all day.
I don't want to miss my Friday fun.

Hey! I'm not hot anymore.
I'm so happy I want to dance.
Mom says I must dance very slowly.
She doesn't want me to get sick again.

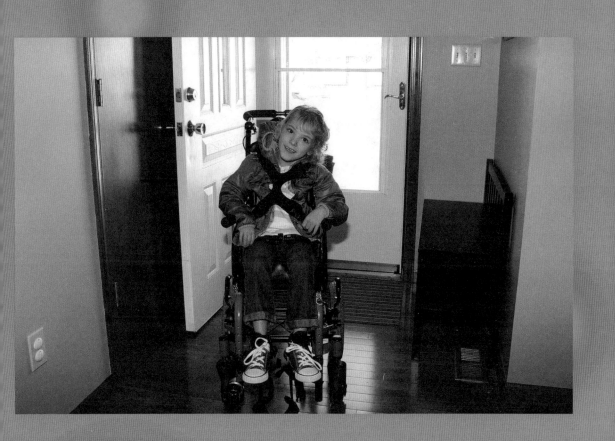

Finally, it's Friday!
I had a great day at schol.
I have some big news.

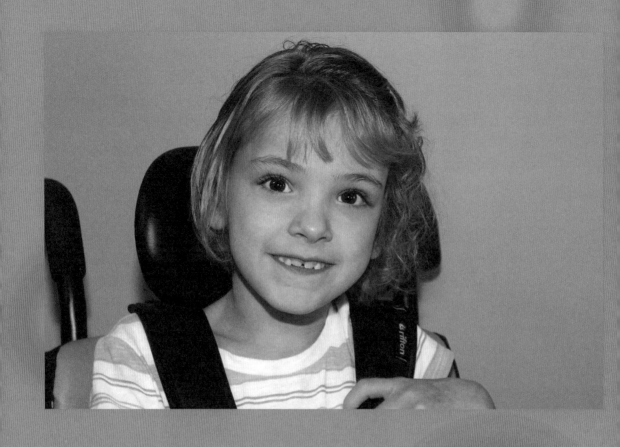

I got 100% on my spelling test.

Now it's time for super fun.
Dad and I are going to the gym.

Dad helped my sisters and brother
play sports.
My sport is boccia.

This is Austin.
He's my coach.
I'm so lucky.
He's a world famous boccia player.

I need to get ready.
I need a ramp.
Should I pick the black one?
Or should I pick the white one?

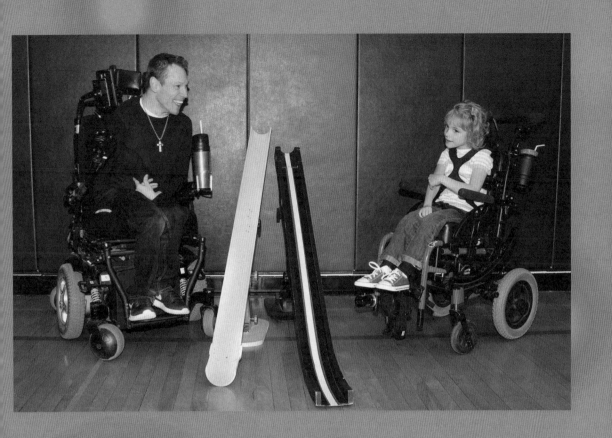

Austin helps me pick the black ramp.
He knows which is best for me.

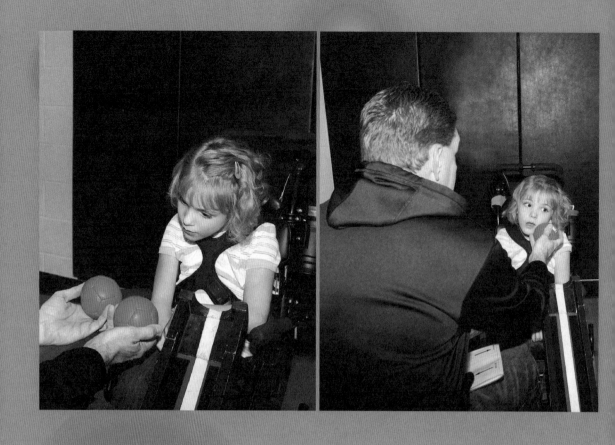

Dad helps me learn about my boccia balls.
Some are soft.
Some are hard.
He helps me feel how they are different.

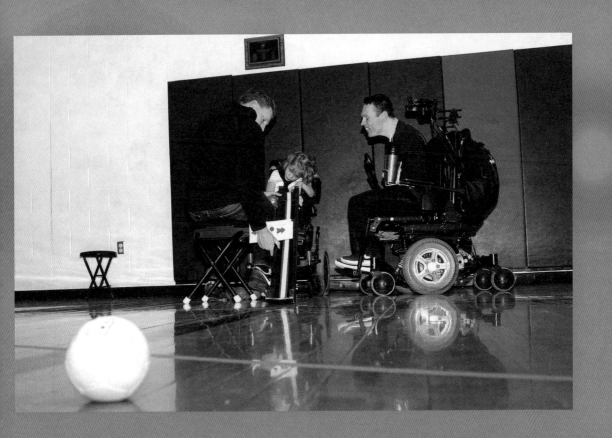

I roll out the ball called the Jack.
That's the white ball.

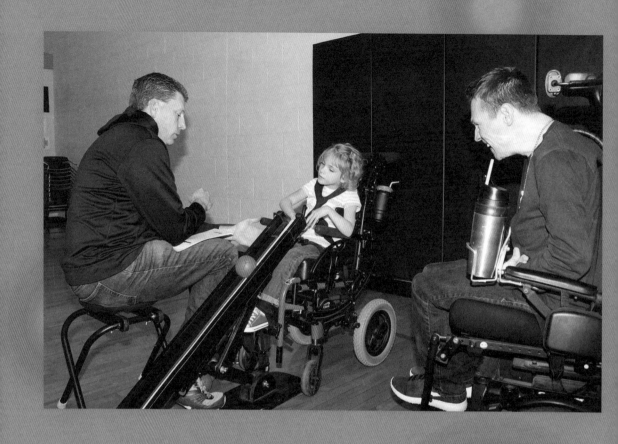

I try to get my boccia balls to kiss the
Jack.
That means my boccia balls touch the
Jack.
The balls closest to the Jack get more
points. That's how you win boccia.

Austin helps me plan my shot.
He tells me to move my ramp to the right.

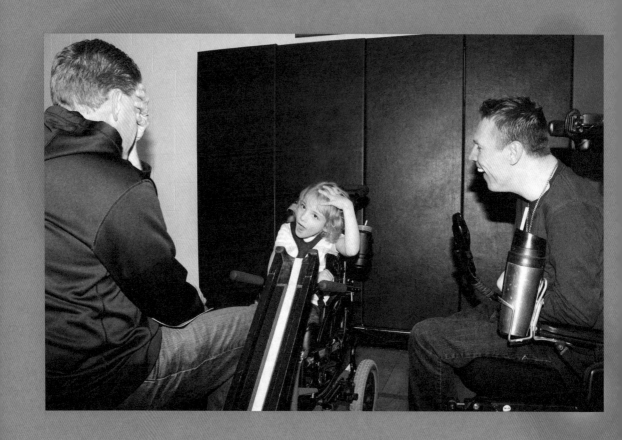

Oh, no, my ball went too far!
The hard ball I picked went too fast.

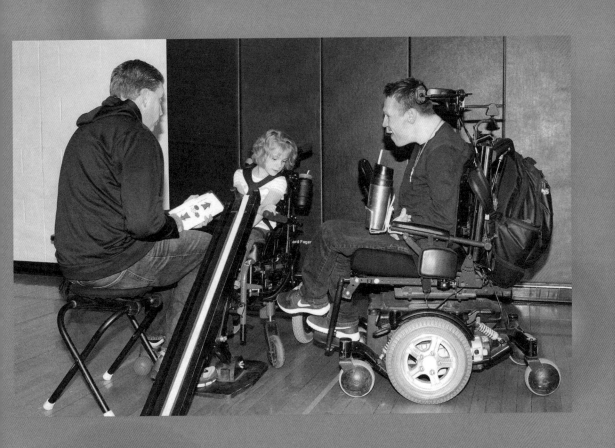

Austin tells me to use a softer ball.
He tells me to move my ramp down.
Austin lightly kicks my chair.
He needs me to listen.

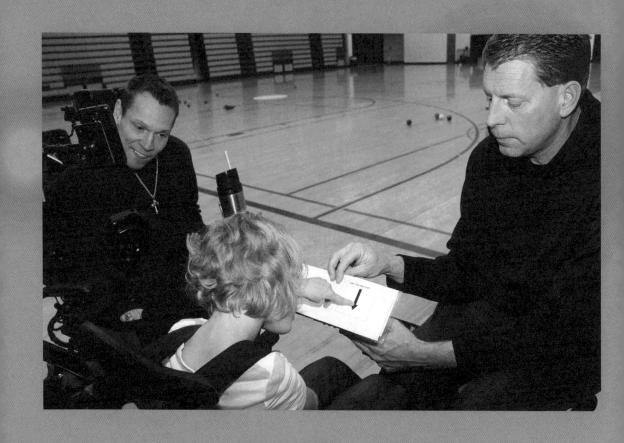

I tell dad to move my ramp down.
I pick a soft ball.
I try again.

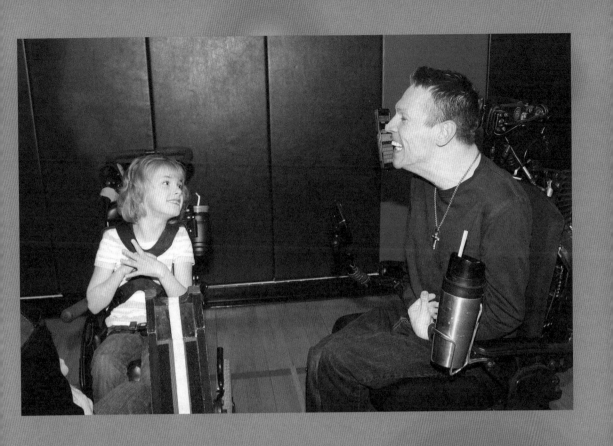

That was better!
My ball got closer to the Jack.

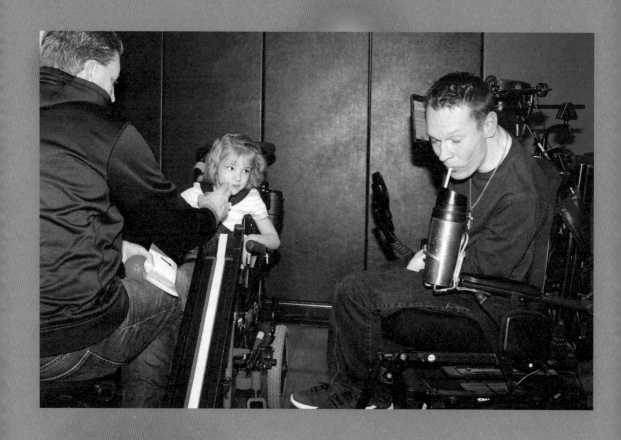

Boccia is hard work.
Austin says it's time for a break.
I have a drink, just like Austin.

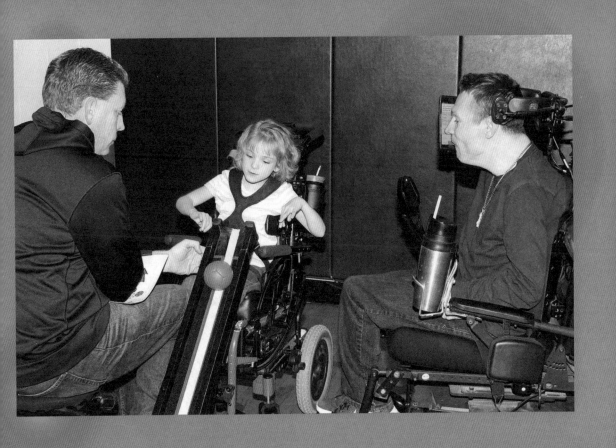

I'm ready for more practice.
I'm going to kiss the Jack.
I want to be as good as Austin someday.

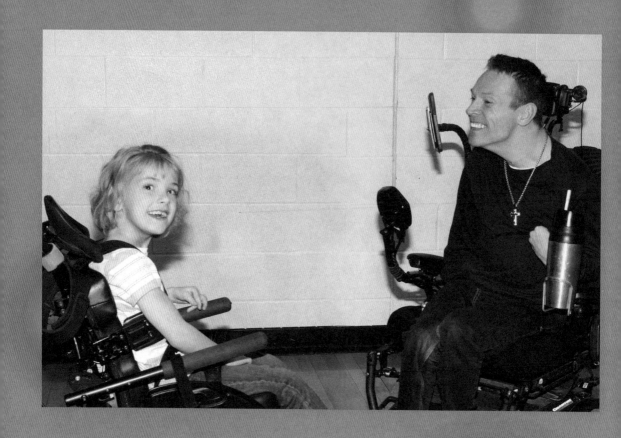

I love to play boccia.
It's so fun with Dad and Austin.
Friday's are the best day ever!